TEAM SPIRIT ®

SMART BOOKS FOR YOUNG FANS

THE COLORADO ROCKIES

BY
MARK STEWART

NORWOOD HOUSE PRESS
CHICAGO, ILLINOIS

Norwood House Press
P.O. Box 316598
Chicago, Illinois 60631

For information regarding Norwood House Press, please visit our website at:
www.norwoodhousepress.com or call 866-565-2900.

All photos courtesy of Getty Images except the following:
SportsChrome (4, 10, 23, 35 top, 36, 41),
Topps, Inc. (7, 22, 29, 33, 34 bottom left, 35 bottom left & right, 40),
Tom DiPace (9, 11, 14, 24, 25), Black Book Partners Archives (45), Matt Richman (48).
Cover Photo: Justin Edmonds/Getty Images

The memorabilia and artifacts pictured in this book are presented for educational and informational purposes,
and come from the collection of the author.

Editor: Mike Kennedy
Designer: Ron Jaffe
Project Management: Black Book Partners, LLC.
Special thanks to Topps, Inc.

Library of Congress Cataloging-in-Publication Data

Stewart, Mark, 1960-
  The Colorado Rockies / by Mark Stewart.
    p. cm. -- (Team spirit)
  Includes bibliographical references and index.
  Summary: "A Team Spirit Baseball edition featuring the Colorado Rockies
that chronicles the history and accomplishments of the team. Includes access
to the Team Spirit website, which provides additional information, updates
and photos"--Provided by publisher.
  ISBN 978-1-59953-480-0 (library : alk. paper) -- ISBN 978-1-60357-360-3
(ebook) 1. Colorado Rockies (Baseball team)--History--Juvenile literature.
I. Title.
  GV875.C78S837 2012
  796.357'640978883--dc23
                                              2011047944

Manufactured in the United States of America in North Mankato, Minnesota.
196N—012012

COVER PHOTO: The Rockies celebrate a victory in 2011.

TABLE OF CONTENTS

ABOUT OUR GLOSSARY

In this book, there may be several words that you are reading for the first time. Some are sports words, some are new vocabulary words, and some are familiar words that are used in an unusual way. All of these words are defined on page 46. Throughout the book, sports words appear in **bold type**. Regular vocabulary words appear in ***bold italic type***.

MEET THE ROCKIES

There is almost never a dull moment when you go to a Colorado Rockies game. The hitters blast baseballs all over the park. The pitchers throw hard and dare opponents to swing. The runners dive headfirst into the bases. The outfielders climb the walls trying to snatch home runs.

The Rockies are a true hometown team. They believe in finding promising young players and training them in the **minor leagues**. When they are ready for the **major leagues**, they join the team in Colorado. Because so many Rockies have "grown up" together, there is a family feeling in the dugout.

This book tells the story of the Rockies. They are one of baseball's newest teams, but they have already made a lot of history. Fans in Colorado have seen lots of record-smashing moments and fantastic finishes. They cheer for their team no matter what the score, because they know the Rockies will never quit.

The Rockies greet Troy Tulowitzki as he returns to the dugout after a home run.

GLORY DAYS

April 9, 1993 was a glorious day for the people in Denver, Colorado. It was the first home game ever for the Colorado Rockies, one of two new teams added to the **National League (NL)** that year. By the time the first pitch was thrown, the Rockies had set a record for the largest Opening Day crowd ever. When all the spectators were counted, there were 80,277 at the stadium. The Rockies sold 4,483,350 tickets in 1993. That also set a record.

To say that fans in Colorado were happy to have their own big-league baseball team only tells part of the story. The Rockies rewarded their support by bringing in some of the game's best hitters, including Andres Galarraga, Dante Bichette, Vinny Castilla, and Charlie Hayes. They treated the fans to one great offensive performance after another.

Unfortunately, the pitching was another matter. Colorado pitchers struggled when they took the mound at home. The air in Denver

CHARLIE HAYES
ROCKIES

is thinner and drier than in most of the country. That helped fly balls travel farther than usual. Many hits that would have been caught for outs elsewhere banged against the fences in Colorado—or flew over them. The Rockies played their outfielders extra deep. But this left open spaces in front of them. That meant short hits often dropped safely for singles and doubles. Being a pitcher for the Rockies wasn't an easy job.

Of course, the Colorado batters loved to play at home. They hit for very high averages and slugged home runs at a record-breaking pace. Many players who wore a Rockies uniform for just a couple of seasons enjoyed the best years of their careers—including Ellis Burks, Juan Pierre, Jeffrey Hammonds, Preston Wilson, and Charles Johnson.

Slowly but surely, the Rockies learned how to gain an edge on their home field. They had a winning record in just their third season and made it to the **playoffs** as the NL **Wild Card**. It was quite a season for Colorado. That same year, the team opened a new stadium.

The stars of the 1995 club included Galarraga, Bichette, Castilla, Larry Walker, and Walt Weiss. Walker became one of the best players in baseball. He won three batting championships, earned five **Gold Gloves**, and was named the league's **Most Valuable Player (MVP)**. In 1997, a hot-hitting rookie named Todd Helton joined Walker in the lineup. The pair gave Colorado a great one-two

punch for many seasons. Helton developed into a superstar slugger and a great fielder. He was the leader of the Rockies as they built a new team for the 21st century.

In 2007—and again in 2009—Colorado won the NL Wild Card. Nothing could match the excitement provided by the 2007 team. That year, the Rockies captured the **pennant** and played in their first **World Series**. Helton was now the experienced leader of a club that included dangerous hitters such as Troy Tulowitzki, Matt Holliday,

LEFT: Todd Helton watches another hit drop in.
ABOVE: Larry Walker was an important leader on the 1995 team.

Brad Hawpe, and Garrett Atkins. In the years that followed, they were joined by Dexter Fowler, Carlos Gonzalez, and Seth Smith.

Meanwhile, Colorado was having more success on the mound at home. The Rockies learned to develop pitchers who were comfortable in Colorado's thin air. The team welcomed many talented arms, including Aaron Cook, Jeff Francis, Ubaldo Jimenez, Jorge de la Rosa, Jhoulys Chacin, Rafael Betancourt, and Huston Street.

The Rockies decided the best plan was to build a team around Tulowitzki and Gonzalez. Both were great all-around players.

"Tulo" won Gold Gloves at shortstop and hit with great power. "CarGo" had a smooth, powerful swing. He loved to chase down balls in the outfield. They shared a passion for winning.

Now the Rockies begin each season knowing they have a chance to return to the World Series. The names and faces on the roster may change, but everyone in Colorado knows that the team has what it takes to compete for a championship. That includes the fans, who continue to support the Rockies with great heart and passion.

LEFT: Troy Tulowitzki cheers on his teammates.
ABOVE: Carlos Gonzalez follows the flight of the ball.

HOME TURF

The Rockies spent their first two seasons in Mile High Stadium. It was also home to the Denver Broncos football team. Fans loved the Rockies and showed it by attending games in record-setting numbers.

In 1995, the Rockies moved into a new ballpark, which was built for baseball. Fans fell in love with the stadium immediately. It had an old-time feel but included many modern touches.

Fans, especially young ones, have a blast at the Rockies' ballpark. There are games and activities all over the stadium. The seats in center field are known as the Rockpile. A solid line of purple seats stretches around the stadium. Each of these seats measures exactly one mile above *sea level*.

BY THE NUMBERS

- The Rockies' stadium has 50,445 seats.
- The distance from home plate to the left field foul pole is 347 feet.
- The distance from home plate to the center field fence is 415 feet.
- The distance from home plate to the right field foul pole is 350 feet.

Fans fill every seat in the stadium during the 2007 World Series.

DRESSED FOR SUCCESS

The Rockies have worn several different uniforms since their first season in 1993. They had one design with sleeveless shirts. One thing that hasn't changed is the team's color combination. The Rockies have always used purple, black, and silver. For some games, the players wear a solid black or solid purple jersey. The most popular style features **pinstripes**.

The team's **logo** looks the same as it did in the early 1990s. It shows a baseball flying through the Rocky Mountains. Like Colorado's uniforms, the logo also uses purple. The team's cap features *CR* in bold letters. In some years, the *CR* has appeared on the players' socks, too.

LEFT: Dexter Fowler wears Colorado's 2011 road uniform.
ABOVE: Walt Weiss fields a grounder in the team's 1993 home uniform.

WE WON!

When the Rockies played their first season in 1993, their fans quickly learned how much fun they would have cheering for their team. Colorado filled the batting order with sluggers. Fans nicknamed their club the "Blake Street Bombers." In 1995, Andres Galarraga, Vinny Castilla, Larry Walker, and Dante Bichette each hit more than 30 home runs. In just their third season, the Rockies made it to the playoffs.

After 1995, the Rockies kept looking for hitters who would do well in Denver's thin air. In the seasons that followed, Colorado scored a lot of runs, but the team failed to reach the playoffs again. In fact, most years the Rockies had a losing record.

The Rockies soon decided to rebuild their team with young players. It took

a few seasons, but by 2007, Colorado had an awesome team. The Rockies fought hard all year long and tied for the NL Wild Card. They then beat the San Diego Padres in a one-game playoff to move on in the **postseason** against the Philadelphia Phillies.

Jeff Francis pitched Colorado to a 4–2 victory in the opening game against the Phillies. One day later, Troy Tulowitzki and Matt Holliday hit home runs in the first inning, and Colorado went on to win Game 2 by a score of 10–5. The Rockies took the third game 2–1 to sweep the series.

Next came the Arizona Diamondbacks in the **National League Championship Series (NLCS)**. The first team to win four games would be NL champions and go to the World Series. In Game 1,

LEFT: Jeff Francis winds up for a pitch during the 2007 playoffs.
ABOVE: Willy Taveras makes a diving catch in Game 2 of the 2007 NLCS.

Francis pitched well again, and the Rockies won 5–1. Game 2 was an exciting contest that lasted 11 innings. Outfielder Willy Taveras saved Colorado with a diving catch in the seventh inning. Later, he pushed home the winning run when he drew a walk with the bases loaded.

The series moved from Arizona to Colorado for Game 3. With the home crowd cheering loudly, the Rockies won 4–1. The winning hit was a home run by Yorvit Torrealba in the sixth inning. The Colorado catcher was not known for his power hitting, but like many Rockies, he played his best when the team needed him most.

The Rockies' ballpark was rocking in Game 4. The team exploded for six runs in the fourth inning. Holliday hit a three-run home run to cap off the scoring. In the ninth inning, relief pitcher Manny Corpas slammed the door shut, and the Rockies were NL champions.

The Rockies were a hot team. Unfortunately, they met a club in the World Series that was playing even better. The Boston Red Sox swept Colorado in four games. Rockies fans were still happy. They knew they had been treated to a very special performance by a very special team.

LEFT: Yorvit Torrealba celebrates his home run against the Arizona Diamondbacks.   **ABOVE**: The Rockies congratulate Matt Holliday after his homer in Game 4 of the NLCS.

GO-TO GUYS

To be a true star in baseball, you need more than a quick bat and a strong arm. You have to be a "go-to guy"—someone the manager wants on the pitcher's mound or in the batter's box when it matters most. Fans of the Rockies have had a lot to cheer about over the years, including these great stars …

 ## THE PIONEERS

ANDRES GALARRAGA — First Baseman

• BORN: 6/18/1961   • PLAYED FOR TEAM: 1993 TO 1997

Andres Galarraga was known as the "Big Cat" for his quickness and grace in the field. However, it was his hitting that made him a favorite of Colorado fans. In his first year with the team, he won the NL batting championship with a .370 average.

DANTE BICHETTE — Outfielder

• BORN: 11/18/1963   • PLAYED FOR TEAM: 1993 TO 1999

Dante Bichette hit for a good average and had excellent power. He was also one of the team's best baserunners. In 1995, Bichette just missed winning the **Triple Crown** with a .340 batting average, 40 home runs, and 128 **runs batted in (RBIs)**.

VINNY CASTILLA　　　　　　　　　　Third Baseman

- BORN: 7/4/1967　　• PLAYED FOR TEAM: 1993 TO 1999, 2004 & 2006

Vinny Castilla was one of Colorado's most popular players. He hit 40 or more home runs three years in a row for the Rockies during the 1990s. In 2004, Castilla returned to the club after four years away and led the NL with 131 RBIs.

ELLIS BURKS　　　Outfielder

- BORN: 9/11/1964
- PLAYED FOR TEAM: 1994 TO 1998

Ellis Burks was a great hitter who had the best season of his career with the Rockies in 1996. That year, he hit .344 with 45 doubles, 40 home runs, and 128 RBIs. He also scored 142 runs and stole 32 bases.

LARRY WALKER　　　Outfielder

- BORN: 12/1/1966
- PLAYED FOR TEAM: 1995 TO 2004

Larry Walker was the best all-around player the Rockies ever had. He was an amazing hitter, excellent fielder, and a smart baserunner. In 1997, Walker hit .366 with 49 homers and 33 stolen bases. He was named NL MVP that year.

RIGHT: Ellis Burks

TODD HELTON   First Baseman

• BORN: 8/20/1973   • FIRST YEAR WITH TEAM: 1997

Todd Helton took over first base from Andres Galarraga and won three Gold Gloves. He also led the NL in batting in 2000. Helton was known as one of the sport's nice guys and made friends all over baseball.

MATT HOLLIDAY   Outfielder

• BORN: 1/15/1980   • PLAYED FOR TEAM: 2004 TO 2008

Matt Holliday was a great football player in high school, but he decided that baseball was his best sport. Colorado fans were thrilled with his choice. In 2007, Holliday batted .340 with 36 home runs and 137 RBIs, and led the Rockies to the NL pennant.

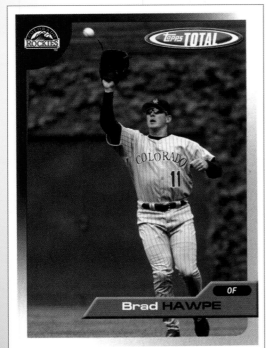

BRAD HAWPE   Outfielder

• BORN: 6/22/1979

• PLAYED FOR TEAM: 2004 TO 2010

Brad Hawpe had a reputation for doing well under pressure. He led his teams to championships in high school and college. The Rockies hoped he could help them build a winning club. Hawpe had his best season in 2007 when Colorado went to the World Series.

CARLOS GONZALEZ   Outfielder

- BORN: 10/17/1985
- FIRST YEAR WITH TEAM: 2009

The Rockies traded Matt Holliday to get Carlos Gonzalez. In his second year with the club, CarGo led the NL with 197 hits and won the batting championship. He also won his first Gold Glove and topped the league in **total bases**.

UBALDO JIMENEZ   Pitcher

- BORN: 1/22/1984
- PLAYED FOR TEAM: 2006 TO 2011

Ubaldo Jimenez was the most exciting pitcher in team history. He had two different fastballs and threw both close to 100 miles per hour. In 2010, Jimenez won 19 games and pitched the first **no-hitter** in team history.

TROY TULOWITZKI   Shortstop

- BORN: 10/10/1984   • FIRST YEAR WITH TEAM: 2006

When Troy Tulowitzki arrived in Colorado, fans were told he was a great all-around player. He lived up to those expectations in 2010 and 2011. Both years, Tulo was voted the best hitting and fielding shortstop in the league.

LEFT: Brad Hawpe   **ABOVE**: Ubaldo Jimenez

CALLING THE SHOTS

Managing the Rockies is one of baseball's toughest jobs. Not every player can be successful in Colorado, which makes building a good team very tricky. It comes as no surprise that the managers who have done well also happen to be some of the most admired people in baseball.

Don Baylor managed the Rockies to 440 wins from 1993 to 1998. He had been the MVP of the **American League** and played in the postseason seven times. Baylor was the perfect leader for a new team. Jim Leyland took over for Baylor in 1999. Two years earlier, Leyland had won the World Series with the Florida Marlins.

In 2002, the Rockies hired Clint Hurdle as their manager. He had

been the team's batting coach. His job was to turn the team's young stars into champions. Hurdle understood what it took to "grow up" in the big leagues. During the 1970s, he was a young player with a bright future. Hurdle learned that it takes hard work and improvement every day to be a star. As a manager, he led the team to its first World Series.

In 2009, after a slow start, the Rockies replaced Hurdle with Jim Tracy. The players loved Tracy's style. He was upbeat and positive. No matter what the score was, he never gave up. Colorado turned its season around. The Rockies ended up winning 92 games. They made the playoffs as the NL Wild Card, and Tracy was named Manager of the Year.

LEFT: Clint Hurdle   **ABOVE**: Jim Tracy

No team was on more of a roll during the final month of the 2007 season than the Rockies. They won 14 of their final 15 games to finish with 89 victories—just enough to tie the San Diego Padres for the NL Wild Card. An extra game was scheduled to decide who would move forward in the playoffs and who would go home.

More than 48,000 fans jammed into Colorado's stadium to cheer for the Rockies. They saw one of the greatest games in history. Yorvit Torrealba and Todd Helton launched home runs to give Colorado the lead. The Padres fought back. In the seventh inning, Garrett Atkins hit a ball that looked like a home run, but the umpires ruled that it had not cleared the fence. They made Atkins stop at second base. Instead of being ahead by two runs, the Rockies led 6-5. The Padres scored in the eighth inning to tie the game.

The two teams battled into extra innings. In the top of the 13th, the Padres went ahead 8–6. Down to their last three outs, the Rockies faced Trevor Hoffman. He had **saved** more games than any pitcher in history.

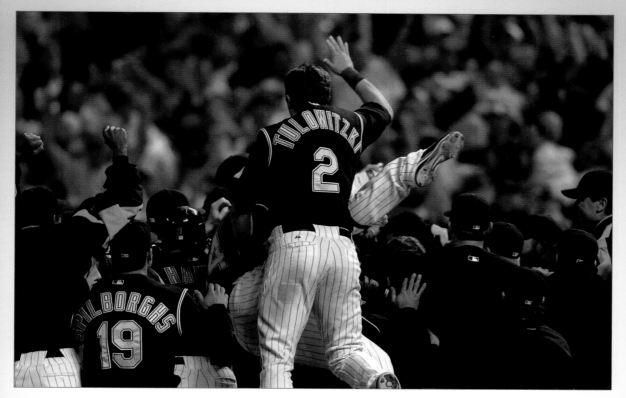

The Rockies go wild after their incredible win over the San Diego Padres.

The fans jumped to their feet when Kaz Matsui lined a double off Hoffman. Troy Tulowitzki followed with a double of his own to drive in Matsui. Next up was Matt Holliday, who legged out a triple that tied the score at 8–8.

Jamey Carroll then hit a fly ball to right field. Holliday tagged up and raced toward home. He slid headfirst and touched home plate an instant before he was tagged by catcher Michael Barrett. The umpire saw this and gave the safe sign. The Rockies were Wild Card champions. They won 9–8 on one of the most exciting plays anyone could ever remember!

LEGEND HAS IT

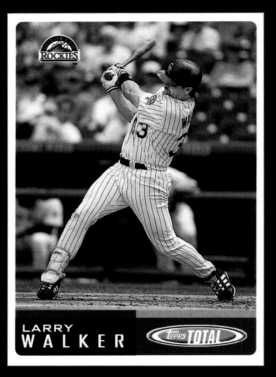

LARRY
WALKER

Topps TOTAL

WHO WAS THE ROCKIES' BEST HOME-FIELD HITTER?

LEGEND HAS IT that Larry Walker was. The Rockies' stadium is known as a great ballpark for hitters. The ball carries very well when it soars high in the thin air, and there is a lot of room in the outfield for hits to drop in. Many Colorado hitters bat better than .300 at home. Nobody enjoyed playing in the Rockies' stadium more than Walker. In 1999, he led the NL with a .379 batting average. Walker did his best work in Denver, where he hit a whopping .461.

ABOVE: Larry Walker
RIGHT: Todd Helton throws a pass for the University of Tennessee.

28

WHICH ROCKIE ONCE LOST HIS JOB TO FOOTBALL STAR PEYTON MANNING?

LEGEND HAS IT that Todd Helton did. Helton was the starting quarterback at the University of Tennessee in 1994. He injured his knee in a game and was replaced by Manning, who was a *freshman* at the time. By the time Helton's knee healed, it was too late—Manning was "the man" at Tennessee.

DO THE ROCKIES LOVE TO HIT AGAINST THE CHICAGO CUBS?

LEGEND HAS IT that they do. Can you blame them? During the 8th inning of a 2010 game, the Rockies set an all-time record with 11 hits in a row against Chicago. Among them were home runs by Ian Stewart and Dexter Fowler. The Rockies scored 12 runs in the inning to win 17–2. Eleven years earlier, the Rockies had another historic day against the Cubs. During a 1999 game, Colorado scored at least one run in all nine innings. The Rockies were only the third team in the 20th century to do that.

Infielders have to be ready for anything. Before each pitch, they scan the field and determine what they'll do if the ball is hit to them. Troy Tulowitzki had a lot on his mind in the seventh inning of a tie game in Colorado in 2007. The Atlanta Braves had runners on first and second with no outs. They had a chance to take the lead.

Kelly Johnson was leading off second base, and Edgar Renteria was leading off first. There were no outs, and Chipper Jones was at bat. The count reached three balls and two strikes. The runners took off on the next pitch, and Jones slammed a line drive up the middle.

Tulowitzki darted to his left and snared the ball in the web of his mitt for one out. He cut toward second base and stepped on it before Johnson could get back there. That made two outs. Tulowitzki looked up to see Renteria, who was caught far off first base. The young shortstop tagged him for the third out. It was just the 13th unassisted triple play in history.

"It kind of just fell into my lap, but I'll take it," Tulowitzki said after the game.

Troy Tulowitzki tags Edgar Renteria for the third out of his unassisted triple play.

Matt Holliday, Colorado's left fielder, told reporters that he had been thinking about a triple play an instant before Jones hit the ball. "Not that I predicted it or anything," he said. "I was just thinking that, so it was kind of weird. I watched it unfold right before my eyes."

TEAM SPIRIT

nyone who doubts the loyalty of Rockies fans should take a stroll around the stadium before a game. Team colors are everywhere. Fans gather at restaurants to talk about Colorado's chances. The license plates on the cars show how far some people will travel to root for the Rockies. Fans come from Kansas, Nebraska, Wyoming, and New Mexico. They visit in the heat of summer, and they visit when the snowflakes are falling in early spring and fall.

Colorado fans attend games in great numbers. In some seasons, the Rockies have sold twice the number of tickets as other teams in the league. For people who live in and around Denver, the stadium is easy to get to. For people coming from outside the state, there are lots of outdoor activities to do before and after games. Indeed, for many, a Rockies game is just one part of a Colorado vacation.

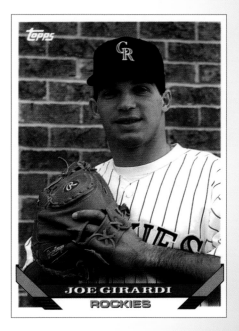

LEFT: Fans come from five different states to watch the Rockies play.
ABOVE: This trading card from the team's first season shows catcher Joe Girardi.

TIMELINE

Ellis
Burks

1993
The Rockies play
their first season.

1996
Ellis Burks leads
the NL in total bases.

1995
The Rockies win the
NL Wild Card.

1997
Larry Walker
wins the MVP.

1998
The **All-Star Game** is played
at the Rockies' stadium.

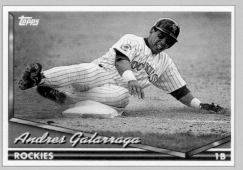

Andres Galarraga
was the star of
the 1993 Rockies.

Denver football star
John Elway takes a
swing during a 1998
All-Star Game
celebrity contest.

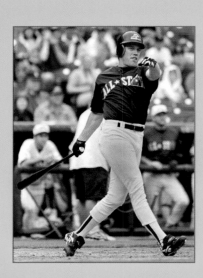

Troy
Tulowitzki

2005
Matt Holliday ties a team record
with eight RBIs in a game.

2010
Carlos Gonzalez wins
the NL batting crown.

2000
Todd Helton wins
the NL batting title.

2007
The Rockies win
their first pennant.

2011
Troy Tulowitzki wins
his second Gold Glove.

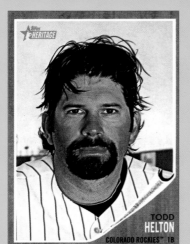

Todd
Helton

Aaron Cook won
eight games for the
Rockies in 2007.

FUN FACTS

NEVER QUIT

In a 2008 game, the Rockies fell behind the Florida Marlins by nine runs. They battled back to win 19–18. The comeback was the largest in Colorado history.

ON SECOND THOUGHT

In the 2009 playoffs, Carlos Gonzalez batted .588 against the Philadelphia Phillies. That was pretty amazing, considering that Gonzalez didn't even start the season with the team. The Rockies sent him to the minors in spring training because they didn't think he was ready to hit big-league pitchers.

Big Blast for the Big Cat

Andres Galarraga hit one of the longest home runs in history against the Florida Marlins in 1997. Some believe it traveled more than 520 feet.

Long and Short of It

The Rockies played their longest and shortest games during the 2008 season. On April 17, they beat the San Diego Padres in a 22-inning game that lasted six hours and 16 minutes. On July 1, they finished a nine-inning game on their home field in one hour and 58 minutes.

Winning Ugly

One of Colorado's best pitchers in the team's early years was Pedro Astacio. He won 42 games from 1998 to 2000. He also gave up 109 home runs during that time!

I Owe You One

When Todd Helton won the batting championship in 2000, he did it with a borrowed bat. Early in the year, he had grabbed one that belonged to teammate Jeff Manto. Helton liked it so much that he used Manto's bats the rest of the season.

LEFT: Carlos Gonzalez bats against the Philadelphia Phillies.

TALKING BASEBALL

"I'm not a guy who is going to make a lot of noise. I hope to lead by example."

▶ **TODD HELTON**, *ON HOW HE INSPIRES HIS TEAMMATES*

"This is my most special moment in thirty-three years in baseball. Nothing can match it."

▶ **JIM TRACY**, *ON MAKING THE PLAYOFFS IN 2009*

"I never want to be satisfied. I always want to get to the next level and help the team improve."

▶ **CARLOS GONZALEZ**, *ON WHAT IT TAKES TO BE ONE OF THE BEST PLAYERS IN BASEBALL*

ABOVE: Todd Helton
RIGHT: Clint Hurdle and Troy Tulowitzki

"Pitching and defense are what win championships."

▶ **CLINT HURDLE**, *ON WHY GOOD HITTING IS ONLY PART OF A SUCCESSFUL TEAM*

"I am thrilled to be in a Rockies uniform for the rest of my career. This is where I want to play. Nowhere else."

▶ **TROY TULOWITZKI**, *ON PLAYING IN COLORADO*

"The ball comes off of his bat as loud and as hard as Larry Walker and Andres Galarraga."

▶ **DON BAYLOR**, *ON THE POWER OF CARLOS GONZALEZ*

"Whatever it takes to get a win, you should be out trying to do it."

▶ **LARRY WALKER**, *ON ALWAYS LOOKING FOR AN EDGE IN BASEBALL*

GREAT DEBATES

People who root for the Rockies love to compare their favorite moments, teams, and players. Some debates have been going on for years! How would you settle these classic baseball arguments?

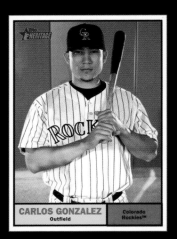

CARLOS GONZALEZ
Outfield
Colorado Rockies™

CARLOS GONZALEZ HAD THE BEST ALL-AROUND SEASON OF ANY COLORADO HITTER ...

… because in 2010 he hit for a high average, with plenty of power and speed. Gonzalez (LEFT) batted .336 to lead the NL and also had 34 homers. For good measure, he added 26 stolen bases—the most on the team. Gonzalez finished the year second in the league in RBIs, third in runs, and fourth in home runs. To top it off, he also won a Gold Glove in center field!

ELLIS BURKS WINS THIS DEBATE ...

… because his 1996 season was truly historic. Burks had a higher average (.344), more homers (40), RBIs (128), and stolen bases (32) than CarGo. He also led the NL in runs scored with 142. That is still a team record. Before Burks had his monster year, the only player ever to have 200 hits, 40 homers, and 30 steals in the same season was Hank Aaron—one of the greatest players in history.

TROY TULOWITZKI HAD THE GREATEST MONTH IN TEAM HISTORY ...

... because in September of 2010 he was unstoppable. With the Rockies fighting for a playoff spot, Tulo came alive in the final month of the season. He hit 15 homers in 30 games and drove in 40 runs. He had two home runs and seven RBIs in one game against the first-place San Diego Padres. The Rockies fell short of winning the **NL West**, but Tulowitzki's "September to remember" was still an amazing month.

NOT EVEN CLOSE! UBALDO JIMENEZ HAD THE BEST MONTH ...

... because in April of that very same season, he might have had the best month of any player on any team— ever! He won twice to begin the 2010 season, and then pitched a no-hitter against the Atlanta Braves. In his next two games, Jimenez (RIGHT) threw two more **shutouts**. He beat the Washington Nationals and Arizona Diamondbacks to finish the month at 5–0. Only one other pitcher in history won five April games and also pitched a no-hitter.

FOR THE RECORD

The great Rockies teams and players have left their marks on the record books. These are the "best of the best" …

ROCKIES AWARD WINNERS

WINNER	AWARD	YEAR
Andres Galarraga	Comeback Player of the Year	1993
Don Baylor	Manager of the Year	1995
Larry Walker	Most Valuable Player	1997
Jason Jennings	Rookie of the Year	2002
Matt Holliday	NLCS MVP	2007
Jim Tracy	Manager of the Year	2009

ABOVE: Larry Walker was named the league MVP in 1997.
RIGHT: Matt Holliday connects with a pitch.

ROCKIES ACHIEVEMENTS

ACHIEVEMENT	YEAR
NL Wild Card	1995
NL Wild Card	2007
NL Pennant Winners	2007
NL Wild Card	2009

ABOVE: Brad Hawpe starred for the 2007 champs.
TOP LEFT: Jeff Francis was also a key player for the 2007 team.
BOTTOM LEFT: Andres Galarraga bumps forearms with Dante Bichette.

PINPOINTS

T he history of a baseball team is made up of many smaller stories. These stories take place all over the map—not just in the city a team calls "home." Match the pushpins on these maps to the **TEAM FACTS**, and you will begin to see the story of the Rockies unfold!

1 Denver, Colorado—*The Rockies have played here since 1993.*

2 West Palm Beach, Florida—*Dante Bichette was born here.*

3 Stillwater, Oklahoma—*Matt Holliday was born here.*

4 Knoxville, Tennessee—*Todd Helton was born here.*

5 Atlanta, Georgia—*Dexter Fowler was born here.*

6 Santa Clara, California—*Troy Tulowitzki was born here.*

7 Philadelphia, Pennsylvania—*The Rockies played in the 2009 playoffs here.*

8 Boston, Massachusetts—*The Rockies played in the 2007 World Series here.*

9 Osaka, Japan—*Kaz Matsui was born here.*

10 Caracas, Venezuela—*Andres Galarraga was born here.*

11 Oaxaca, Mexico—*Vinny Castilla was born here.*

12 Maple Ridge, British Columbia, Canada—*Larry Walker was born here.*

Andres Galarraga

GLOSSARY

🏆 BASEBALL WORDS
🧠 VOCABULARY WORDS

🏆 **ALL-STAR GAME**—Baseball's annual game featuring the best players from the American League and National League.

🏆 **AMERICAN LEAGUE (AL)**—One of baseball's two major leagues; the AL began play in 1901.

🧠 *FRESHMAN*—A first-year college student.

🏆 **GOLD GLOVES**—The awards given each year to baseball's best fielders.

🧠 *LOGO*—A symbol or design that represents a company or team.

🏆 **MAJOR LEAGUES**—The top level of professional baseball. The American League and National League make up today's big leagues; also known as the major leagues.

🏆 **MINOR LEAGUES**—The many professional leagues that help develop players for the major leagues.

🏆 **MOST VALUABLE PLAYER (MVP)**—The award given each year to each league's top player; an MVP is also selected for the World Series and the All-Star Game.

🏆 **NATIONAL LEAGUE (NL)**—The older of the two major leagues; the NL began play in 1876.

🏆 **NATIONAL LEAGUE CHAMPIONSHIP SERIES (NLCS)**—The playoff series that has decided the National League pennant since 1969.

🏆 **NL WEST**—A group of National League teams that play in the western part of the country.

🏆 **NO-HITTER**—A game in which a team does not get a hit.

🏆 **PENNANT**—A league championship. The term comes from the triangular flag awarded to each season's champion, beginning in the 1870s.

🧠 *PINSTRIPES*—Thin stripes.

🏆 **PLAYOFFS**—The games played after the regular season to determine which teams will advance to the World Series.

🏆 **POSTSEASON**—The games played after the regular season, including the playoffs and World Series.

🏆 **RUNS BATTED IN (RBIs)**—A statistic that counts the number of runners a batter drives home.

🏆 **SAVED**—Recorded the last out or outs in a team's win. A relief pitcher on the mound at the end of a close victory is credited with a "save."

🧠 *SEA LEVEL*—The low point used when measuring the height of geographical features, such as mountains.

🏆 **SHUTOUTS**—Games in which one team does not score a run.

🏆 **TOTAL BASES**—A player's total number of bases when you add up all of his hits.

🏆 **TRIPLE CROWN**—An honor given to a player who leads the league in home runs, batting average, and RBIs.

🏆 **WILD CARD**—A playoff spot reserved for a team that does not win its division, but finishes with a good record.

🏆 **WORLD SERIES**—The world championship series played between the AL and NL pennant winners.

EXTRA INNINGS

TEAM SPIRIT introduces a great way to stay up to date with your team! Visit our **EXTRA INNINGS** link and get connected to the latest and greatest updates. **EXTRA INNINGS** serves as a young reader's ticket to an exclusive web page—with more stories, fun facts, team records, and photos of the Rockies. Content is updated during and after each season. The **EXTRA INNINGS** feature also enables readers to send comments and letters to the author! Log onto:

www.norwoodhousepress.com/library.aspx

and click on the tab: **TEAM SPIRIT** to access **EXTRA INNINGS**.

Read all the books in the series to learn more about professional sports. For a complete listing of the baseball, basketball, football, and hockey teams in the **TEAM SPIRIT** series, visit our website at:

www.norwoodhousepress.com/library.aspx

ON THE ROAD

COLORADO ROCKIES
2001 Blake Street
Denver, Colorado   80205
(303) 292-0200
colorado.rockies.mlb.com

**NATIONAL BASEBALL
HALL OF FAME AND MUSEUM**
25 Main Street
Cooperstown, New York 13326
(888) 425-5633
www.baseballhalloffame.org

ON THE BOOKSHELF

To learn more about the sport of baseball, look for these books at your library or bookstore:

• Augustyn, Adam (editor). *The Britannica Guide to Baseball*. New York, NY: Rosen Publishing, 2011.

• Dreier, David. *Baseball: How It Works*. North Mankato, MN: Capstone Press, 2010.

• Stewart, Mark. *Ultimate 10: Baseball*. New York, NY: Gareth Stevens Publishing, 2009.

INDEX

ABOUT THE AUTHOR

MARK STEWART has written more than 50 books on baseball and over 150 sports books for kids. He grew up in New York City during the 1960s rooting for the Yankees and Mets, and was lucky enough to meet players from both teams. Mark comes from a family of writers. His grandfather was Sunday Editor of *The New York Times,* and his mother was Articles Editor of *Ladies' Home Journal* and *McCall's.* Mark has profiled hundreds of athletes over the past 25 years. He has also written several books about his native New York and New Jersey, his home today. Mark is a graduate of Duke University, with a degree in history. He lives and works in a home overlooking Sandy Hook, New Jersey. You can contact Mark through the Norwood House Press website.